I looked up, and there I sa... his
tummy and his toes touching the...
wasn't walking in his sleep, he was floati...
it!

YOUNG CORGI BOOKS

Young Corgi books are perfect when you are looking for great books to read on your own. They are full of exciting stories and entertaining pictures and can be tackled with confidence. There are funny books, scary books, spine-tingling stories and mysterious ones. Whatever your interests you'll find something in Young Corgi to suit you: from ponies to football, from families to ghosts. The books are written by some of the most famous and popular of today's children's authors, and by some of the best new talents, too.

Whether you read one chapter a night, or devour the whole book in one sitting, you'll love Young Corgi books. The more you read, the more you'll want to read!

Other Young Corgi books to get your teeth into:
BLACK QUEEN by Michael Morpurgo
LIZZIE ZIPMOUTH by Jacqueline Wilson
SAMMY'S SUPER SEASON by Lindsay Camp
ANIMAL CRACKERS by Narinder Dhami

Billy the Bird

Dick King-Smith

Illustrated by John Eastwood

YOUNG CORGI

Also available by Dick King-Smith,
and published by Young Corgi Books:

All Because of Jackson   The Guard Dog
Connie and Rollo   Horse Pie
ESP   Omnibombulator
Funny Frank

BILLY THE BIRD
A YOUNG CORGI BOOK : 0 552 55392 1

PRINTING HISTORY
Doubleday edition published 2000
Young Corgi edition published 2001

Young Corgi Books are published by Random House Children's Books,
61–63 Uxbridge Road, London W5 5SA,
a division of The Random House Group Ltd,
in Australia by Random House Australia (Pty) Ltd,
20 Alfred Street, Milsons Point, Sydney, NSW 2061, Australia,
in New Zealand by Random House New Zealand Ltd,
18 Poland Road, Glenfield, Auckland 10, New Zealand
and in South Africa by Random House (Pty) Ltd,
Isle of Houghton, Corner of Boundary Road & Carse O'Gowrie,
Houghton 2198, South Africa.

Printed and bound in Great Britain by
Cox & Wyman Ltd, Reading, Berkshire.

Chapter One

I was four, nearly five, when my brother
Billy was born. I was ever so excited. I'd
been longing for a baby brother, or
sister, I didn't care which. Dad said he'd
quite like a son, Mum said she didn't
mind, another daughter would do just as
well. Both of them said it didn't matter
which it was, as long as it was a normal
healthy happy baby. Which is just what
Billy appeared to be. But neither of
them had the faintest idea (and they still
don't) that though Billy was (and still is)
healthy and happy, he is definitely not
normal.

I didn't find out till he was four and I was eight, nearly nine. It was a warm summer evening, Friday, 20 June in fact, a date I shall never forget. I'd said goodnight to Mum and Dad and gone upstairs, and on my way to my bedroom I peeped into Billy's room, as I always did, just to see he was all right. His bed was empty.

At first I wasn't too worried. He must have gone to the loo, I thought. But he wasn't in the bathroom, nor in Mum and Dad's room, nor anywhere else. He must be sleepwalking, I thought, I must go and tell them. But first I had another look in Billy's room in case he'd come back from his sleepwalk. But the bed was still empty.

Then suddenly I heard, above my head, a small snore. I looked up, and there I saw Billy, his nose, his tummy and his toes touching the ceiling. He wasn't walking in his sleep, he was floating in it!

You must have all seen pictures on the telly of astronauts inside their space-craft, in orbit beyond the Earth's atmosphere, floating about light as feathers. You must have thought what fun it would be, to be able to do that. But of course, because of the pull of gravity, it's not possible, down here on

Earth, for anyone to become weightless. Not possible, that is to say, for any normal person.

I remember staring up at my little brother with my mouth wide open like a fish. I remember the pyjamas he was wearing, blue ones with a pattern of pink rabbits. I remember thinking, thank goodness for the ceiling, otherwise who knows how high he might have gone. I remember closing the window very quietly in case he might float out through it, and seeing, as I did so, that the moon had just risen, and that it was a full moon, huge and round and creamy.

I turned back from the window to see my little brother dropping back down again, fat arms and legs spread like a starfish, and landing softly on his bed, still fast asleep.

I must tell Mum and Dad, I thought, and then I thought, No, I won't, they won't believe me anyway. I'm going to keep it a secret. For one thing's certain, my girl, I said to myself: there may be millions of girls called Mary, and probably thousands of Marys that have little brothers called Billy. But I bet I'm the only girl in the world who has a brother who is able to become weightless.

Chapter Two

Next morning I talked the whole thing over with my guinea pig, Mr Keylock. He's named after the greengrocer in whose shop we buy carrots and stuff for him. Both of them have big red moustaches. People say that animals can't talk. That's not true, lots of them can, and guinea pigs are specially chatty. You've just got to learn all the different languages.

I was so anxious to get Mr Keylock's opinion about what had happened that I didn't feed him straight away, as I usually do. I wanted to know what he thought. I was sure I would understand whatever he said, you nearly always can if you take the time to listen to animals properly.

Now, for example, when I spoke to him, he chattered back at me and I was pretty sure what he was saying.

"Do you know what Billy did, last evening?" I asked Mr Keylock.

"No," he said.

"He flew up to the ceiling!"

"Oh."

"Don't you think that's extraordinary?"

"Yes."

"D'you think I should tell Mum and Dad?"

"Up to you."

What's the matter with him this

morning, I thought? He's not saying
much. Then I realized. I hadn't fed him
yet. "Would you like a carrot?" I said.

"Yes, yes, yes, yes!" squeaked Mr
Keylock. "I thought you'd never ask."

He tucked into that carrot so greedily
that there wasn't much point in saying
any more to him till he'd finished.

When he had, I said, "It's a bit of a
joke, Billy flying, isn't it? Considering his
name, I mean." (Our surname is Bird,
you see.)

13

"You must have been dreaming," Mr Keylock said.

"I wasn't."

"You must have been. Humans can't fly, any more than pigs can. Or guinea pigs."

So I decided to ask Lilyleaf about it. Lilyleaf is our cat, rather old and very wise, and the first thing she said to me when I told her about Billy flying was, "Does he know that he flew?"

"I haven't asked him," I replied.

"Well don't," said Lilyleaf, "and don't tell him what happened. If he believes he can fly, he'll be jumping out of the window to try it."

So I didn't say anything to my little brother about it. But every evening when I looked into his bedroom, I half expected (half hoped, really) that he'd be floating up against the ceiling. But he never was, not until Sunday, 20 July, and this time he wasn't asleep. As soon as I came into the room, he called down to me from the ceiling. "Look at me, Mary!" he cried excitedly.

I rushed to shut the window. Now Billy rolled over and then pulled with his arms and kicked with his legs like a swimmer and flew all round the room. Just then the cat came in and Billy called to her, "Look at me, Lilyleaf, I'm flying!" and he turned a somersault in the air. Then he swooped down and landed back on his bed, light as a feather. He put his head on his pillow and shut his eyes and went straight back to sleep.

"The first time he flew," said Lilyleaf,
"the moon was full, remember?"

"Yes."

"As it is now."

"You mean, he can only do it at full
moon?"

"I think so," said Lilyleaf. "It's only
then that Billy can defy gravity. When's
the next one?"

We went to my room and I looked in my diary that I keep by my bed. "The next full moon," I said, "will be on Monday August the eighteenth."

"Then that's when he'll fly next," said Lilyleaf.

Usually the summer holidays whizz by, but now the time seemed to go, oh, so slowly as I waited for Billy's next scheduled flight. I did think again about telling Mum and Dad, but I could just imagine the conversation:

MARY. Mum, Dad, I think I should tell you. Billy can fly.

DAD. Rubbish!

MUM. Don't be silly, darling.

MARY. But he can! Honestly! We saw him, all of us, Lilyleaf, Mr Keylock and me.

MUM. You've been dreaming, Mary. Only birds can fly.

DAD [laughing]. Don't forget – Billy *is* a Bird!

MARY [becoming impatient]. But he
        can, he can!
DAD AND MUM TOGETHER [becoming
        angry]. Oh do stop it, Mary.
        Don't be so stupid and try to
        be more truthful. Yes, shut up,
        please.

So I didn't say anything to them but
at least I could talk about it with the
cat and the guinea pig. Lilyleaf, I was
sure, would want to be there when the
time came, and so would Mr Keylock:
he made me promise to take him
upstairs to watch.

So at last, on the evening of 18
August, the three of us made our way
up to Billy's bedroom, and, lo and
behold, there he was, already flying
around – Billy the bird!

"Hullo, Mary!" he cried as he
swooped over our heads. "Hullo,
Lillyleaf! Hullo, Mr Keylock!"

My heart was thumping, and Mr

Keylock's red moustaches bristled, and Lilyleaf's green eyes glowed as we watched. So fascinated were we that I quite forgot to close the window, and suddenly Billy flew out through it, and away.

Chapter Three

I rushed to the window, carrying my guinea pig, and the cat jumped up on the sill, and we all three stared out to see Billy flying silently away.

Mum and Dad were sitting on the swing-seat on the lawn, enjoying the evening sunshine. Dad was reading his newspaper, Mum her book. "Oh help!" I whispered to Lilyleaf. "I hope to goodness they don't look up!"

"Neee-o," she said, or that's what it sounded like.

Mum didn't notice, but at that very moment, just as Billy went swooping

over their heads, Dad took off his glasses
to clean them and looked up into the
sky while he was doing this.

"Gosh!" he said to Mum. "Did you
see that?"

"What?" Mum asked.

"A blooming great big bird flew over us just then."

"What was it?" Mum asked.

"Couldn't see it properly, I was cleaning my glasses, but it was ever so big."

It wasn't, I thought. It was a little Bird.

Just then Mr Keylock began to squeal loudly, the squeal which I knew meant, "Come on, I'm starving, for goodness' sake feed me."

At this Mum and Dad looked up and
saw us all at Billy's bedroom window.

"Is Billy asleep?" Mum called.

"Well . . . no," I said.

"Not surprised," said Dad,
"considering the row that greedy animal
of yours is making."

"Come on downstairs now, Mary,"
said Mum. "I'll be up in a minute to say
goodnight to Billy."

Help! I thought. What shall I do? But
then I saw Billy coming gliding back
over the lawn as silently as an owl, while
in the evening sky behind him the full
moon, I could see, was already rising. In
through the window Billy swooped and
onto his bed and into it. He lay there
grinning at us.

"That was lovely fun, Mary!" he said.

"You gave us all an awful fright," I
said.

I looked out of the window. Mum was
getting up from the swing-seat to come
into the house. Quickly I bent over
Billy's bed.

"Listen," I said
to him. "Listen,
Billy, this is
important.
Mum's coming
up to say good-
night, and we're going to have to tell her
that you've been flying. If Dad had had

his specs on just now and seen you, he might have had a heart attack."

But already my little brother was fast asleep, tired out, I supposed, by his flight. Mum came in.

"He's asleep now," I said.

"I should hope so," she said, looking at her watch. "I hadn't realized it was so late. Goodness, how time flies."

And that's not the only thing that's been flying, I said to myself. I didn't sleep very well that night. I lay in my bed, thinking of Mum and Dad sleeping soundly in theirs, and Billy in his. Mr Keylock would be in the land of dreams, dreams of food of course, and only Lilyleaf would be awake, hunting out in the dark night. Every time I was just dropping off, I started to worry. Should I tell Mum and Dad what Billy had done?

I'd told him we should but he'd already gone to sleep. I'll tell him again first thing in the morning, I thought. I looked at my watch. One o'clock, morning already! I must have slept then because when I looked at my watch again it was half past six.

People say that if you have to make a big decision, it's best to sleep on it first. Well, I had, hadn't I, and now I began to feel differently. It looked pretty certain that my little brother could only fly at the time of the full moon, and the next one, my diary said, was not until 16 September, twenty-nine days away. No point in telling Mum and Dad yet, was there? Anyway, I didn't want them to worry.

I got out of bed and tiptoed along the passage to Billy's room. Gently, I shook him awake. "I've been thinking," I said. "Perhaps we'd better not tell them."

Billy rubbed his eyes. "Don't know what you mean," he said.

"About you flying."

"*Flying?*" said Billy, yawning. "What d'you mean? People can't fly, only birds can."

"But you did! In June and in July and again yesterday evening."

"Oh, don't be silly," said Billy. "Go away and leave me alone."

After my breakfast I went down the garden to Mr Keylock's hutch to give him his. Lilyleaf followed. "Look," I said to them both. "I wasn't dreaming last night, was I? Billy did fly, didn't he?"

"No doubt about it," said the cat.

"And Mr Keylock, you saw him too?"

"Yes, yes," said the guinea pig, "and for goodness' sake,

girl, don't stand there holding that carrot, give it here, I'm starving!"

I gave it to him and Lilyleaf and I watched him pitching into it as if he hadn't been fed for a fortnight.

"The point is," I said to Lilyleaf, "that this morning I was saying to him that perhaps we shouldn't tell Mum and Dad about it, about him flying I mean, and he didn't seem to know what I was talking about."

"That figures, Mary," said Lilyleaf. "He can only fly on the night of the full moon, and what's more, only then does he know that he *is* flying. At any other time he's just an ordinary little boy, quite unaware of this gift that he has."

"That must be it!" I said. "Lilyleaf, you *are* clever."

"I know," said the cat in her smug way.

The guinea pig bolted the last of his carrot and squeaked for more in his greedy way.

As we walked back up the garden Lilyleaf said to me, "Better have a look in your diary."

"Why?" I asked.

"Find out when the next full moon is."

"I know that," I said. "On September the sixteenth."

"And what about the other ones, this year?"

"Let's see . . . October the sixteenth

 . . . and then November the fourteenth . . . and then December the fourteenth."

Chapter Four

By 16 September I'd decided, after a lot
of thought, to allow Billy to fly outside.
It's cruel to keep a caged Bird, I thought.
By a slice of luck on 16 September
Mum and Dad had some friends to supper, so there was little risk of them
seeing Billy the Bird in action. By the
time they'd said goodbye to their visitors
and come upstairs to make sure my
brother was asleep, he was. How amazed
they would have been to have heard
what he'd told us when he'd returned.

"That was brill!" he said. "It was ace!
It was mega! I flew right up over the

town. Our house looked tiny from up there."

"I hope no one looked up and saw you," Lilyleaf said. "The evenings are still quite light. Someone might have spotted you."

What none of us knew then was that someone had. The local evening newspaper on 17 September had a piece which caught Dad's eye. "Listen to this," he said to Mum, and he read it out.

SIGHTING OF UFO

Several people have reported the sighting of an unidentified flying object high above the town at approximately 8.30 pm yesterday evening. It has been variously described as looking like a large bird or a small microlight, though some were convinced that the UFO was an alien from another planet. Most unlikely of all was one person's belief that the figure was that of a small child. Pigs might fly!

"Honestly!" Dad said. "Some people will believe anything! Of course it was a bird. Probably the same one that flew over last month, remember?"

Later I told Lilyleaf about the piece in the newspaper. "At least it'll be darker next month," I said, "now winter's coming."

"Better not open his window till after it's dark," Lilyleaf said. "It'd be the safest time too, as your mum and dad will be asleep."

"But how will Billy see his way around?" I said. "Cats can see in the dark but people can't."

"They can if it's a full moon," said Lilyleaf. "It'll be almost as bright as daylight."

But at both the next two full moons – 16 October and 14 November – the weather was cold and very wet, so I kept the window shut and Billy had to be content with flying round the room until I hit on the idea of opening his door and letting him fly down the passage and round Mum and Dad's room and my room and the bathroom, to make it more of an outing for him. Lilyleaf stood guard at the head of the stairs to give warning if Mum or Dad should come out into the hall below.

Which they did do, once, during the
November flight, and the cat gave a
loud, "Miaouw!" and Billy came skim-
ming back down the passage at top
speed and into bed.

"What was Lilyleaf making that
noise for?" they said when they came
up.

"She wants her supper, I expect," I said.

"I want mine!" squealed Mr Keylock.
"I'm starving!"

"Put the creature
back in its hutch,
Mary," Dad said.
"It'll wake Billy."

"It won't!" I said, because I'd seen my
little brother's eyelids flicker and I knew
that this time he wasn't asleep, just pre-
tending. When Mum and Dad had gone
back downstairs, I whispered to him,
"Good boy, you didn't tell them."

"Tell them what?" Billy said.

"That you can fly."

"Course I didn't," he said. "It's a secret
between you and me and Lilyleaf and
Mr Keylock," and he shut his eyes again
and fell fast asleep.

But when I said to him next morning,
"Gosh, you're getting fast, Billy! You
flew along the passage like a swallow!",
he only said, "Oh you and your silly
dreams."

Chapter Five

It was a Sunday on 14 December so
Dad was at home, and Mum made him
start on the Christmas decorations. He
grumbled, saying there was loads of
time, another eleven days yet. But in
fact he rather enjoys fixing up all the
fairy lights (he's a DIY man), not just
on the Christmas tree but all over the
front of our house too. There's no mis-
taking the Birds' nest at Christmas time
– it's far and away the brightest house
in the whole street.

Once it was dark, Dad switched all
the lights on – just to make sure they

were working – and they were. We all
went outside and they looked lovely, all
different colours, and some that winked
and blinked, and one lot – bigger,
golden ones – that were fixed so as to
say: MERRY CHRISTMAS.

 Of course there
was a very big
golden light up
in the sky too,
the full moon,
and I suddenly
thought, Oh
help, suppose Billy just takes off now, in
front of everyone!

But in fact he went to bed and
straight to sleep and when it was my
bedtime he was still soundly asleep. So I
made sure his window was closed and I
drew the curtains to keep out the moon's
bright light, and
then I shut his
bedroom
door,
leaving
Lilyleaf
on
guard
outside it.

"Wake me if you hear him moving," I said to her. Perhaps he won't fly tonight, I thought to myself as I was drifting off, perhaps he doesn't fly every full moon, perhaps he's lost the trick of it. But the next thing I knew was someone saying, "Psssst" in my ear.

"I can hear him," Lilyleaf said. "He has lift-off."

We found Billy doing warm-up circuits of the room.

"Quietly, Billy," I whispered to him. "We don't want to wake up Mum and Dad", and then I put some warm clothes on him over his pyjamas (it was December, after all) and went to open the window. "Don't be long," I said to Billy the Bird, "and try not to let anybody see you."

We sat waiting by the window. I was yawning like mad, longing to go back to sleep, but Lilyleaf, being a creature of the night, was wide awake and just as I was dozing off, she went, "Psssst" in my ear again.

"Here he comes," she said, and in sailed my little brother.

"Good flight?" I said.

"Mega," said Billy.

"Anyone see you?"

"No, but I saw someone."

"Who?"

"A burglar."

"How d'you know he was a burglar?"
I asked.

"Well," said Billy, "he was climbing
up the side of one of those old houses in
Quiet Street. I landed on the roof of a
house opposite and watched."

"Climbing up a ladder, you mean?"

"No, he was climbing up the ivy on
the wall and when he got to an upstairs
window he opened it with something
and slipped inside."

"A cat burglar," Lilyleaf said.

"Oh no!" I said. "Oh Lilyleaf, just
suppose he breaks into our house and
steals you!"

"No," she said. "A cat burglar is someone who is very nimble and agile and stealthy and clever and good at climbing up things. Just like a cat."

I wonder if it'll be in the evening newspaper, I thought next day, and later I sneaked a look at Dad's copy while he was watching the telly, and it was!

YET ANOTHER DARING ROBBERY!

The latest in what is now a long line of burglaries occurred in the early hours of this morning. An intruder broke in through an upper window of 22, Quiet Street, and stole a quantity of jewellery without disturbing the members of the household. As with previous thefts, no ladder appears to have been used and it is presumed that the man climbed the ivy on the house wall in the classic manner of cat burglars.

Only then did it strike me that our house walls are covered in ivy!

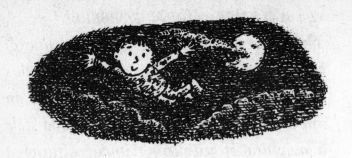

Chapter Six

At breakfast I said to Dad, "Did you see that bit in last night's paper? About the burglar?"

"Yes," he said.

"Well, our house is covered in ivy. He might climb up our walls next. He could, easy, he's a cat burglar."

Dad laughed. "Afraid he'll steal Lilyleaf?" he said. "I shouldn't worry too much about it, Mary, especially just now. With all my fairy lights, ours is the most brightly lit house in town, I should think. Anyone would be able to see a cat burglar climbing up our walls." He got up from the table. "I'll be a bit late back this evening," he said to Mum. "The usual Monday meeting of the Ways and Means Committee, and I'm in the chair."

When he'd gone off to work I said to Mum, "What do people do at a meeting?"

"Oh, they talk about things."

"What are 'ways and means'?"

"Oh, how to do things."

"What did Dad mean – he's going to be in the chair? Do all the others have to stand up?"

"You and your endless questions, Mary," Mum said. "It means he's the chairman, he's in charge of the meeting."

When I got back from school that Monday afternoon, I said to Lilyleaf, "We're going to have a meeting. In the living room", and I went down the garden to fetch Mr Keylock from his hutch and told him.

"Eating, did you say?" he asked.

"No," I said. "Meeting."

I came back and sat in Dad's big armchair. Billy was watching children's TV and Mum was busy in the kitchen. The guinea pig sat on my lap and the cat lay along the arm of the chair.

"Right then," I said to them. "This is a meeting of the Ways and Means Committee. I'm in the chair."

"Any fool can see that," said Mr
Keylock in a grumpy voice, "but I
haven't had my tea."

"Ways and means of what?" Lilyleaf
said.

"Of protecting this house against that
cat burglar."

Mr Keylock didn't exactly prick up his ears (he can't) but he said, "He doesn't nick guinea pigs, does he?"

"No, nor cats. But he steals jewellery and stuff, and he does climb like a cat. Billy saw him. What I'm asking this committee is, how do we find ways and means of guarding against him? Mr Keylock?"

"No good asking me," said the guinea pig. "I sleep at night, like all sensible creatures."

"I don't," said Lilyleaf, "and I'm also more sensible than some I could mention. I can be on patrol outside."

"But how would you give warning?" I said.

"Make a terrible horrible awful row, I suppose," said Lilyleaf. "It's a pity that Billy only flies once a month. He'd be the ideal guard. Just imagine, that old burglar  would have forty fits if he suddenly saw Billy the Bird."

Mum came in. "Tea's nearly ready," she said to me, ("I wish mine was," squeaked Mr Keylock) and to Billy she said, "Turn that thing off."

"But it's my favourite programme," he said.

"Well turn it off as soon as it's over," she said, and to me, "Have you done your homework?"

"No," I said. "We've been having a
meeting. I'm in the chair."

"You're a funny girl," said Mum. "You
jabber away to those two animals as
though they could understand what you
mean. Tea in ten minutes," and she went
out of the room.

Mr Keylock set up an angry chattering and Lilyleaf began to purr loudly, and it was easy enough for me to understand what they meant. The guinea pig was annoyed because he hadn't had his tea, and the cat was amused because the guinea pig was annoyed. As for me, I was worried because the meeting of the Ways and Means Committee hadn't got us anywhere.

"I'm worried," I said to Lilyleaf that night. She was lying on my bed as she often did before going downstairs and through the cat-flap for a night's hunting. She got up and stretched and rubbed her furry face against mine, purring softly as if to say, "Don't worry, it may never happen."

And in fact it didn't; Christmas came and went, and Dad took down the fairy-lights, and the New Year began. Perhaps the cat burglar was too busy enjoying himself, thanks to all the valuable things he must have stolen, but there had been no more reports of thefts by the time the January full moon rose.

Once again Billy slept later than he had done in the summer and autumn full moons, and it was after midnight when Lilyleaf went, "Pssst," in my ear before going off on patrol.

"Listen, Billy," I said to him when I'd got him dressed up ready for take-off. "Fly along above as many streets in the town as you can, specially where there are houses with ivy or Virginia creeper on them, and see if you can spot that burglar again. Stealing things is wrong, he should be stopped."

"What do I do if I see him?" Billy asked.

"Make a terrible horrible awful row,"
I said, "to wake people up. But don't let
them see you. Fly straight home."

"OK," said my little brother, grinning,
as I opened the window. "Watch out,
burglar! Here comes Billy the Bird!"

Chapter Seven

When he'd flown away, I shut the
window and sat in a chair beside it,
ready to let him in again on his
return. With no Lilyleaf to wake me –
she was on patrol outside – of course I
fell asleep. I was suddenly woken by
not one but two terrible horrible
ghastly rows. One row came from
Lilyleaf, caterwauling in the street
below, and the other seemed to be just
above the bedroom window. I opened
it and looked out to see a sight I shall
never forget. No more than two metres
below me, under the window, clinging

to the ivy, was the figure of a man dressed
all in black and wearing a black hood.

I looked upwards, and there above
the window hovered Billy, making a
selection of hideous faces, sticking his
fingers in his ears, poking his tongue
out, crossing his eyes, and letting out the
most weird noises that sounded like,
"Ah! Wah! Gah! Gummygummygummy!
Wollywollywoo!"

Then, louder even than boy or cat, the man let out a great yell of terror, lost his grip on the ivy, and fell, landing on our lawn with a horrid thump.

"Come in, quick, Billy," I called, and then I shut the window and pulled off the extra clothes he was wearing and popped him into bed and scuttled off to my own room.

I lay there, hearing Dad and Mum go rushing down the stairs, and then came the noise of a lot of people talking excitedly outside. Last came the *nee naw! nee naw!* of sirens, first of a police car and then of an ambulance.

I got up and went and looked in Billy's room but he was soundly asleep despite all the rumpus, so I went downstairs too.

"Whatever's happening?" I said to Mum and Dad, who were standing on the lawn in their dressing-gowns, talking to neighbours. Everyone seemed very agitated. "What do you think, Mary?" Dad said. "It's that cat burglar?"

"He must have been climbing up our wall and he fell off," Mum said. "Oh, he

60

made such terrible noises!"

"They're just loading him into the ambulance," Dad said.

"Come on, Mary," said Mum. "Back to bed," and she came upstairs with me and went on into Billy's room.

"Can you believe it!" she said when she came back. "He slept right through all that terrible horrible ghastly row! Never knew anything about it! You go back to sleep, there's a good girl."

Before I did, Lilyleaf came in and jumped up on my bed, purring like mad. "A good night's work" she said. "I think I'll have a cat-nap."

When I woke up the next morning, I lay imagining another conversation.

MARY. Billy *did* know about it.

MUM. How could he have done? It didn't even wake him.

MARY. He was awake all right. Long before the noise woke you up. He frightened the cat burglar so much that he fell off the ivy.

DAD.   Whatever do you mean?

MARY.   Well, he hovered right above
        the man, making faces and
        awful noises.

DAD.   What d'you mean, he hovered?

MARY.   I told you before. He can fly.
        Like a bird.

DAD AND MUM TOGETHER [becoming
        angry]. Oh do stop it, Mary.
        Don't be so stupid and try and
        be more truthful. Yes, shut up,
        do.

Tuesday evening's newspaper reported:

CAT BURGLAR ARRESTED

In the early hours of this morning, an attempted robbery by the town's now notorious cat burglar ended in his falling from an ivy-covered wall up which he had been climbing. He was taken by ambulance to the Cottage Hospital, where he was found to be suffering from concussion, though otherwise miraculously unhurt. Police are at his bedside.

But Wednesday's report was much fuller . . .

CAT BURGLAR ATTACKED BY ALIEN

The intruder who fell from the wall of a house yesterday has now told the police that he was attacked by an alien. He described his attacker as a monstrous thing the size of a small boy. It had its fingers in its ears and its tongue stuck out from a hideous face, as he could clearly see by the light of the full moon. It flew down out of the night sky, he stated, and hovered above him, cursing him in a foreign language.

Could this be connected with the UFO that was supposedly sighted on 16 September last year? Or was the man's story simply the result of concussion? Throughout, he insisted that the alien was definitely flying. The man has now been taken into custody.

I told Lilyleaf about the pieces in the paper.

"He was lucky not to break his neck," she said. "Perhaps cat burglars have nine lives."

I told Mr Keylock but as usual he only wanted to talk about food. I told Billy the Bird (he hadn't read the newspaper of course — he couldn't).

"Wow!" he said. "An alien! I wish I'd seen the man fall off the wall!"

You did, Billy, I said to myself. You did.

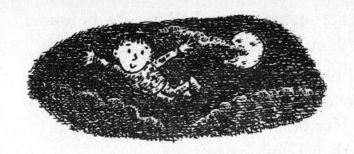

Chapter Eight

"I've had an idea," I said to Lilyleaf and
Mr Keylock.

It was a Saturday morning and I was
cleaning out the guinea pig's hutch as I
always do then. He groans and grumbles

because it means he has to wait longer than usual for his breakfast. Lilyleaf usually comes to watch, wearing an expression which says plainly that it's a pity other animals aren't as clean in their habits as cats are.

"An idea about what?" she said.

"About Billy's next scheduled flight, in February," I replied.

"What idea?" said Mr Keylock. "And hurry up, do, girl, I'm famished."

"Well," I said, "we don't really know where he goes or what he does on these flights. Except for the last one. Usually when he returns, he just goes straight to sleep and then of course next day he doesn't even know he's been flying. If only I could go on a flight with him, but of course he couldn't carry me, I'm much too heavy."

"So am I," said Lilyleaf quickly.

"But aren't you curious to find out what flying would be like?" I said to her.

"Curiosity killed the cat," she replied.
"But you never know, guinea pigs might
fly."

We both turned to Mr Keylock.
"Don't look at me!" he squeaked.

"You don't weigh much," I said to
him. "Billy could easily carry you."

"Billy could easily drop me," said Mr
Keylock.

After I'd put fresh sawdust on his hutch floor and filled his hayrack and his water bottle and given him some cabbage leaves, Lilyleaf and I walked back up the garden together.

"How long do you suppose Billy will go on flying?" I said to her. "Surely he won't still be doing it when he's bigger?

He'll get too heavy to lift off, won't he?"

"Think of those astronauts," the cat said (she'd seen them on the telly, too). "They're weightless, no matter how big they really are."

"So he could still be doing it when he's a grown man as big as Dad?" I said.

Lilyleaf made a sort of chuckling noise and then I began to giggle. Dad is a very big man, a bit on the fat side to be honest, and I had a sudden mental picture of him swooping and soaring above the town like a jumbo jet. How horrified the townspeople would be if they saw the large figure of the Chairman of the Ways and Means committee whizzing over their heads!

"Sooner or later somebody's bound to spot him," I said. "Close enough to see that what they're looking at isn't a UFO or an alien, but a small boy called Bird, flying like one. Then all the world would come to our town, prime ministers and presidents and pop stars, even the Queen perhaps, to see this flying boy, and it'd be in all the newspapers and on the telly and the radio and there'd be film crews everywhere and we'd never have a moment's peace."

None of that had happened as a result of the January flight, because no-one had seen Billy except the cat burglar, and no-one believed *his* story because they thought he was concussed or drunk or mad. But our local evening paper kept on about UFOs and aliens, printing letters from people who believed in one or the other.

He's much more likely to be seen now, I thought, because they'll be looking for him, looking up into skies lit by a full moon. But, luckily I suppose, the weather at full moon was terrible both in February and March, so that Billy

had to be content with flying around indoors. Not till the following month did I allow him to fly out. Once again we worked it so that he didn't take off till well after midnight, but the April full moon was the most brilliant one imaginable. The town was lit up as though by a great searchlight in the sky.

"Someone," I said to Lilyleaf, "is bound to see him this time."

And someone did. Boys will be boys, the saying goes, and Billy could be naughty or silly like all little boys are now and then. I suppose he must have become bored with just flying quietly about and thought he'd amuse himself by giving someone a fright. So he landed on top of the church tower and sat there, dangling his legs. He looked down and there in the street right below him was a man, a man in uniform walking slowly along.

Billy couldn't see that it was a police-

man. He just thought, I suppose, that it'd
be fun to give this man a fright, so he
shouted, "BOO!" How do I know all this?
Because it was all in next evening's paper.

Readers may remember the story which we printed with regard to a burglar who, in January, stated that he had been attacked by an alien, a story which many of you will have considered to be nonsense. Now, however, a further sighting has occurred, this time from a much more reliable source. Our community policeman, PC George Gibbs, made the following report:

"At 1.15 am I was passing St Margaret's Church when I heard a loud shrill cry above me. Looking up, I could see clearly by the light of the full moon a figure, sitting on the very edge of the church tower. I was unable to distinguish its features, but it appeared to be the size of a small child about four years of age. How it came to be there, I had no idea, since the church is kept locked at night and no child could possibly have scaled the tower from the outside, but it was obviously in a position of the gravest danger.

'Don't more!' I called up to it. 'Just stay right where you are. Help is on its way,' and I radioed the police station, requesting them to summon the fire brigade. The appliance arrived at St Margaret's Church at 1.32 am."

As soon as the fire engine arrived, I read, the firemen extended a long ladder to the top of the church tower where the figure was still sitting. However it then disap- peared, presumably moving to the further side.

But when a fireman reached the head of the ladder – the newspaper report went on to say – and climbed onto the flat area on the top of the tower, he found that it was empty. There was no sign of anyone, and a search of the interior of the church and of the church-yard revealed nothing.

Finally, the report concluded . . .

Whatever PC Gibbs had seen on top of St Margaret's Church had vanished into thin air. How can it have done this, human or alien, unless it had the power of flight? Humans do not have this power. Aliens presumably do.

Chapter Nine

I looked up the date of the May full
moon. As usual, it was represented in the
diary, under the due date, by a circle,
like a capital O. Thus: "O. Full moon"
though I did happen to notice that on
this particular date in May it read "OO.
Full moon" and then, in brackets,
"(Lunar eclipse)".

I had no idea what those last two
words meant, so I didn't mention them
to Lilyleaf, in fact I never thought
about them till the actual night. It was
a warm one and Billy flew off after
midnight in his blue pyjamas

with a pattern of pink rabbits.

I stood at the window in the brilliant moonlight, looking at that great round circle in the sky and the pattern of darker marks upon its white surface. Some people thought of it as the face of a man and talked about the Man in the Moon. Some people swore they could see on it the outline of a hare.

As I stared at it, I noticed a curious shadow starting to appear at the lower rim of the circle, as though a curved dark cloud was beginning to

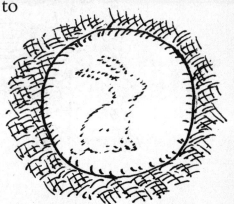

intrude upon the moon's brightness. I
tried to keep on watching, because the
shadow seemed to be getting bigger and
so the moon's light to become less. But I
just couldn't keep awake, until the usual
"Pssst" woke me. I looked out and saw
that only about a quarter of the face of
the moon was still showing.

"Whatever's happening?" I asked
Lilyleaf.

"Didn't it say, in your diary?" she said.

"Say what?"

"That tonight's the night of a lunar eclipse."

"Oh," I said. "Oh yes, but I didn't know what it meant."

"It means," said the cat, "that now and again the full moon enters the shadow of the Earth. Then, before long, that shadow spreads right over the face of the moon and almost blots it out."

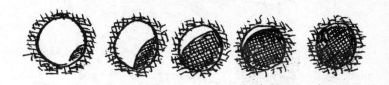

"Blots out its light, you mean? But then how will Billy see to fly back?"

"Let us just hope," said Lilyleaf, "that he is able to fly back. Better open that window, ready."

Just then we heard a sort of thump on the wall outside. It couldn't be that cat burglar, could it, I thought? They locked him up, didn't they?

I looked out and leaned over and there, clinging to the ivy just below the window, was my little brother. "Mary, Mary! Help me!" he cried, and I stretched down and grabbed his arms and somehow managed to pull him up over the window-sill and into his bedroom.

"Whatever's happened?" I said. "Why didn't you just fly in?"

"I couldn't," Billy said. "I was flying really, really high and then it began to get darker and I began to come down, lower and lower, I couldn't help it, and I got so tired I thought I was going to crash-land, but I just managed to cross the lawn and I got nearly up to the window. But then I felt I couldn't fly any more and I grabbed hold of the ivy." He yawned enormously.

"Help me into bed, Mary," he said, and I did, and immediately he fell asleep.

Before I went to my own room, I looked out of Billy's window and saw the last thin gleam of that May full moon disappear, completely covered now, in the lunar eclipse.
All was pitch black.

In the morning Billy, of course, remembered nothing about the drama of the night. Mum and Dad knew nothing about it either. At breakfast Dad opened his daily newspaper and said to Mum, "Fancy! There was an eclipse of the moon last night!"

"I didn't know that," Mum said.

"I didn't know that," Mr Keylock said when I told him.

"Billy started to lose his power of weightlessness," I explained, "because of the full moon being eclipsed. He was lucky not to have crashed."

Just then Billy came down the garden
carrying a dandelion, which he gave to
the guinea pig.

Mr Keylock twiddled his ginger
moustaches. "You're a good boy," he
said. "Even if you never become
weightless again."

"Whatever does he mean?" asked
Billy, as we walked back up the garden.

"You don't remember, do you?" I said.
"Having such a job to get home?
Because of the eclipse?"

"Eclipse?" said my little brother.
"What are you talking about, Mary?"

I sighed. At least you won't miss
flying, I thought, because you've never
known you can. But I shall be very
sorry if you've lost your powers.

"D'you think he will have done?" I
asked Lilyleaf later.

"Who will have done what?"

"Billy. Lost his powers of flight," I
said, "because of the eclipse?"

"Yes," said Lilyleaf, "I do think that. The moon, as all cats know, is a magic body, and your little brother could somehow use that magic, even on cloudy nights. But because the moon was completely blacked out by the eclipse, I believe that may have cut the magic cord that bound Billy to it."

And sadly she was right.

The moon waxed and the moon waned, month by month, but never again, even when it was full, did Billy the Bird defy gravity.

Perhaps it wasn't anything to do with the eclipse, perhaps he'd just grown out of it, but on every date where my diary recorded "O. Full moon" I kept watch in the evening and Lilyleaf did so throughout the night, keeping guard over my little brother, waiting for him to levitate, to rise, just a few centimetres perhaps, a couple of metres, up to the ceiling maybe as he had first done. But he never moved.

"It's no good me telling him all that has happened," I said to Lilyleaf. "He just says I've been dreaming, or thinks I'm mad. Only you and I know the truth. You and I and Mr Keylock."

"And the cat burglar," said the old cat.

One evening the following June, almost exactly a year since Billy's maiden flight, we were all sitting on the swing-seat on the lawn, enjoying the evening sunshine, Mum and Dad and Billy and me and Lilyleaf and Mr Keylock. It was late, well past Billy's bedtime, but it was such a lovely evening that he'd been allowed to stay up.

Suddenly we saw a pale ghostly shape floating across our garden.

"Look!" said Dad. "An owl."

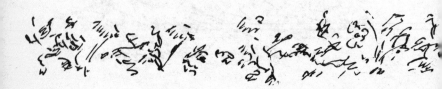

"Oh!" said Mum. "Wouldn't it be wonderful to be able to fly like that!"

"Wouldn't it," said Dad.

"It would," I said.

Lilyleaf began to purr and Mr Keylock gave a grunt.

"People can't fly," my little brother said.

"You're right, Billy," Dad replied. "Because of the force of gravity. A *person* could only fly if he or she was weightless. Like astronauts in a spacecraft, in orbit beyond the Earth's atmosphere."

"I dreamed," I said, and I squeezed Mr Keylock and nudged Lilyleaf, "I dreamed that Billy could fly." (And as I said it, I wondered for an instant, did I dream it all?)

"Me? Fly? Don't be so silly, Mary," said Billy the Bird.

THE GUARD DOG
Dick King-Smith

'Out of his hairy little mouth came the most awful noise you can possibly imagine. . .'

There are six puppies in the pet shop window; five posh pedigree puppies, and a scruffy little mongrel with a grand ambition – to be a guard dog.

The other pups laugh at him. How can such a small, scruffy dog possibly expect to be bought to guard a home? Especially when his bark is the most horrible, earsplitting racket they have ever heard! Will the poor little guard dog be doomed to a lonely life in the Dog's Home – or worse. . . ?

A hilarious tale from Dick King-Smith – Children's Author of the Year, British Book Awards 1991

captivating read for
. . . a winner!'
Bookshelf

52731 9

RBACK ORIGINAL

ilable by post from:
IM99 1BQ. Tel: +44(0)1624 836000,
://www.bookpost.co.uk or
terprise.net

as customers: all £1 per book (paper-
(hardbacks).